Overcoming the Odds:
Sports Biographies

Ali:
The Greatest

by

Alan Venable

Don Johnston Incorporated
Volo, Illinois

Edited by:

Jerry Stemach, MS, CCC-SLP
Speech/Language Pathologist, Director of Content Development, Start-to-Finish® Books

Gail Portnuff Venable, MS, CCC-SLP
Speech/Language Pathologist, San Francisco, California

Dorothy Tyack, MA
Learning Disabilities Specialist, San Francisco, California

Consultant:

Ted S. Hasselbring, PhD
William T. Brian Professor of Special Education Technology, University of Kentucky

Graphics and Illustrations:

Photographs and illustrations are all created professionally and modified to provide the best possible support for the intended reader.

Narration:

Professional actors and actresses read the text to build excitement and to model research-based elements of fluency: intonation, stress, prosody, phrase groupings and rate. The rate has been set to maximize comprehension for the reader.

Published by:

Don Johnston Incorporated
26799 West Commerce Drive
Volo, IL 60073

800.999.4660 USA Canada
800.889.5242 Technical Support
www.donjohnston.com

DON JOHNSTON

International Standard Book Number
ISBN 1-893376-45-1

Contents

4

Chapter 1

"Who Stole My Bike?"

On a Saturday in 1954, a boy was riding his bike in Louisville, Kentucky. He came to a big building where people were giving away free popcorn. The popcorn smelled good, so he parked his bike and went inside. When he came back out, his bike was gone.

"Who stole my bike?" he asked.

No one knew. Everyone told him to ask the police about it.

"Where's the police?" he asked. And he started to cry.

They pointed to the basement of the hall. "There's one cop down there in the gym."

The boy went down the steps. The man in the gym was not dressed like a cop.

"Are you a cop?" asked the boy.

"Yes," replied the man. "My name is Joe Martin."

"Someone stole my bike," said the boy. "I want it back. I'm going to whup the guy that stole it. He'll wish that he was never born."

"Slow down," said Joe. "You better learn how to fight before you tell folks that you're going to whup them!"

The boy looked around. There were other boys in the gym. They were wearing boxing gloves. They were hitting at punching bags.

"Can you teach me how to fight?" the boy asked.

"Yes," said Joe. "If you're good, I can let you box on TV. I run a boxing show for kids on TV here in town."

"I just want to whup that guy who stole my bike!" said the boy.

Joe said, "Come back on Monday night and start training as a boxer. I'll teach you for free. What's your name?" he asked.

"Cassius," answered the boy. "My name is Cassius Clay."

On Monday night Cassius Clay came back to the gym. He got into the ring with an older boy. Pow! Whap! Soon young Clay's head was spinning. His nose was bleeding. Joe dragged him out of the ring.

Another boy put his arm around Clay. "Don't box with the older boys yet. Box with the boys who are new like you. You need to *learn*."

So Clay began to learn how to box. Every night, he went to the gym. At first, Clay didn't seem better than the other new boys. He was tall for his age and he was skinny. He swung his arms like a windmill. But he was quick, and he worked hard. After six weeks, Joe let him box on TV. The fight was three rounds.

Each round was three minutes long.
No one got knocked out, but Clay was
the winner.

After that, Clay worked harder at
boxing than any other boy that Joe had
ever taught. For the next six years,
boxing was the thing that Clay cared
about the most. The Golden Gloves
was a national boxing contest for boys.
Clay thought about the Golden Gloves
all the time. He didn't mix with girls.
He didn't drink beer. He didn't smoke.
He didn't get into trouble. In school, he
dreamed all day about boxing.

Clay's friends wanted him to play football with them. One day, he tried it. Later he said, "They gave me the ball and tackled me. My helmet hit the ground. Pow! No sir. You got to get hit in that game. Too rough! You don't have to get hit in boxing."

That might sound strange, but that was one of young Clay's secrets. He was quick and he had sharp eyes. When someone swung at him, he could move a little backward or move to the side, and the punch would miss him. That was important.

Boxing is a dangerous sport. One punch to your head can hurt you for the rest of your life. One punch can kill you. A boy who gets hit too much in the head doesn't last very long in boxing.

Chapter 2

Young Hero

CORBIS/Bettmann-UPI

In 1960, Cassius Clay won an Olympic gold medal for boxing.

Outside the ring, Clay was always cocky, but he wasn't mean. He made friends with the other boxers. He asked his neighbors to come and watch him box. People liked his smile. He was fun to be around.

By age 18, Clay had grown a lot and he was one of the best young boxers in the United States. He won the Golden Gloves contest. In 1960, he was picked for the summer Olympic Games in Rome, Italy. He had a great time at the Olympics.

He made friends with athletes from all over the world. But he was still shy around girls.

Clay won the Olympic gold medal for boxing in the light heavyweight class. He was very proud. Back in the U.S., he wore his Olympic medal and jacket all the time. Everyone seemed to know who he was now. He was amazed to be so famous. He loved to shake hands with people and give them his autograph. There were parades for him in Louisville.

It was time for Clay to become a pro boxer so that he could earn his living by boxing. But that cost money. Clay needed money to hire a trainer to coach him. He had to rent a gym and pay men to practice with him. And he needed money to travel.

Clay's parents didn't have much money, so he borrowed money from a group of businessmen. After each fight, Clay would get part of the ticket money and maybe some money from TV. At first, it wouldn't be much money. Later it might be more.

For five years, Clay had to share his pay with the businessmen.

Clay wanted to become the heavyweight champ of the world. To do that, he had to beat the current champ. But first, he had to fight other boxers. His trainer would have to help him decide who to fight each time. The businessmen hired a trainer named Angelo Dundee. Angelo knew all about boxing. When Angelo and Clay met, they liked each other, so Angelo became Clay's trainer. For the next 20 years, they were a team.

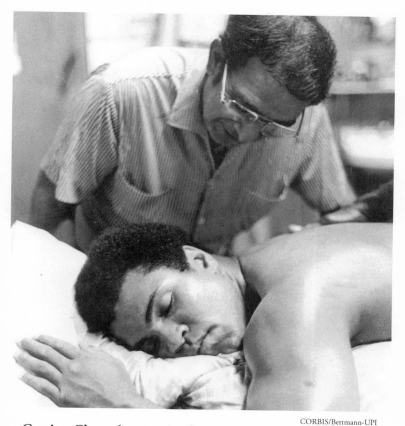

CORBIS/Bettmann-UPI

**Cassius Clay takes a rest after training.
Angelo Dundee, his trainer, is standing nearby.**

Angelo gave Clay ideas about how to punch and how to defend himself. He taught Clay not to use up too much energy early in a fight.

Angelo wasn't bossy. He didn't say, "Do this, do that." He respected Clay. He always let Clay decide what to do in a fight. He let Clay push himself. Angelo said that Clay was like a jet plane that wanted to fly. All Angelo had to do was to flip a switch and Clay would take off.

Clay's first pro fight was in October, 1960. The other boxer was a policeman from a small town. He was not a great boxer, and Clay beat him without much trouble. Each boxer got $2,000. After the fight, the policeman said, "Some day Cassius Clay will be the champion of the world."

Clay did well in his first fights as a pro. Before each fight, he went out and asked people on the street to come to the fight. More people meant more money. But mostly, Clay just wanted to have people watch him box.

He bragged a lot. That got more people to come. It also made Clay feel bigger. And it might make the other boxer feel smaller.

Clay said strange things before a fight. He made up poems about himself. Here is his shortest poem:

Me!

Wheeeeeeeee!

People thought he was silly. Who ever heard of a boxer who was a poet? But he was fun to watch. And he was a fine boxer.

Chapter 3

The Beautiful Boxer

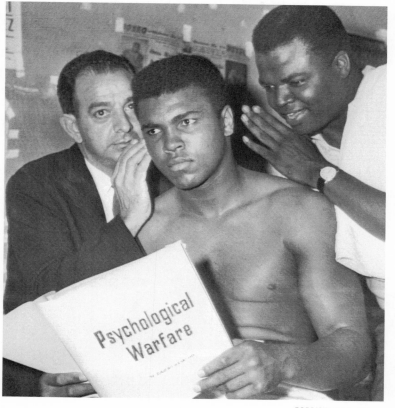

CORBIS/Bettmann-UPI

Cassius Clay gets ready to fight Sonny Liston.

Back then, athletes were not supposed to show off. Football players didn't dance like chickens. Basketball players didn't do fancy slam dunks. Athletes just did their jobs for their teams. But Cassius Clay broke all those rules.

"I am so pretty!" he bragged. "I am so beautiful!"

Whoever heard of a beautiful boxer? Boxers were not supposed to be beautiful. But Cassius Clay was saying something different.

In those days, black people didn't talk in public about being beautiful. Miss America had to be white. Big movie stars had to be white. America didn't call black people beautiful.

But Clay was proud to be a handsome African-American. He was proud to say, "Look at me. I am beautiful."

Clay was speaking for all black people. He was saying, "We have a right to say how beautiful we are. We have a right to be happy about ourselves."

From 1960 to 1963, Cassius Clay won many fights. In 1964, it was time for him to fight a man named Sonny Liston for the heavyweight crown. Sonny Liston was a powerful boxer. He had been boxing for more than ten years. He had also been in jail. One time he was in jail for armed robbery. Another time it was for beating up a policeman. Sonny Liston was mean and angry. Other boxers said that he had an evil eye.

Before the fight, Clay said things to tease Liston and to make him nervous.

UPI/CORBIS-Bettmann

Cassius Clay points to the home of heavyweight champion Sonny Liston.

People said that only a crazy person wouldn't be afraid of Sonny Liston. So Clay started acting and talking crazy. He wanted Liston to think that Cassius Clay was a crazy man.

Clay said, "Sonny Liston can't talk. Sonny Liston can't fight. The man needs talking lessons. The man needs boxing lessons. He's going to fight me, so he needs *falling* lessons, too. I'm gonna be champion of the whole universe. After I whup Sonny Liston, I'm going to whup those little green men from Mars.

I won't be afraid to look at them because they won't be uglier than Sonny Liston."

Clay told the reporters, "Sonny Liston is a big ugly bear. He's too ugly to be the world champ. The world champ should be pretty like me. After I whup Sonny Liston, I'm going to give him to the zoo!"

Some people make bets on boxing. They were betting seven dollars to one dollar that Liston would beat Clay. But Clay kept screaming about beating Liston. Clay really *did* sound crazy!

When Clay was training to fight Sonny Liston, the Beatles came to his gym. Clay pretended to knock them all out with one punch. Clay loved to be a clown in public.

But in private, Clay was more serious. Something big was happening to him. It had to be kept secret before the fight. Cassius Clay's family was Christian. His mother had taught him all that she knew about God and about what was right. She taught him to love people and treat everyone with kindness.

She had taught him not to hate anyone. And that was how Clay was. When he wasn't being a boxer, he always respected other people.

But Clay was choosing a new religion. He was becoming a Muslim. Muslims belong to a religion called Islam. Islam started in Arabia about 600 years after Jesus. The Muslim word for God is Allah. Their holy book is called the *Koran*.

Muhammad Ali talks to other Black Muslims in 1968.

Good Muslims pray five times every day. They don't smoke or drink. Islam also teaches the same things as most other religions. Islam says that people should love each other.

Chapter 4

Sting Like a Bee

CORBIS/Bettmann-UPI

Cassius Clay went to the United Nations in 1964 to meet with important leaders.

There are different kinds of Muslims. Cassius Clay had joined a Muslim group called the Nation of Islam. Some people called them the "Black Muslims." The Black Muslims didn't let white people join them. Other Muslim groups are open to all races. The Nation of Islam said that white people were devils who had stolen the world from the black people. The Nation of Islam said that blacks shouldn't mix with whites. They said that it was better to be equal but to live apart.

Clay didn't believe everything that the Nation of Islam said, but he believed a lot of it. He was 22 years old then. He was angry about how black people were treated in the U.S. Even an Olympic hero like Clay was sometimes treated badly because he was black. He was not allowed to eat in some restaurants. He couldn't stay in some hotels.

Clay respected Martin Luther King. But he liked the way that the Nation of Islam spoke about being angry with white people.

At first, Clay couldn't tell anyone that he had become a Muslim because the people who were in charge of pro boxing might find out about it. They didn't like the Nation of Islam, so they might call off the fight.

Before each fight, there was a big meeting. At the meeting, each boxer had to show that he was the right weight for his class. A doctor had to make sure both boxers were healthy.

Clay came to the meeting shouting like a madman. "Float like a butterfly, sting like a bee! I'm the champ! I'm ready to rumble! Bring me that big ugly bear!"

A doctor checked Clay's heart. It was beating too fast. The doctor said that Clay was "scared to death, and might crack up before the fight." Everyone thought that Clay was so scared that he was crazy.

The fight between Clay and Liston was set to be 15 rounds long. Each round would last three minutes.

Cassius Clay looks like a madman as he fights Sonny Liston.

At the fight that night, Clay *was* scared in round one. After that, he felt much better. He saw that he could duck away from Liston's fists. He could keep from getting hit too much. In round three, Clay started to attack Liston. Clay's hands were so fast that Liston couldn't see them coming. Clay hit Liston in the face and made a cut under Liston's eye. The trainer put oil on the cut to stop the bleeding.

In round four, Clay's eyes began to hurt. Some of the oil had gotten into his eyes.

Probably the oil from Liston's cut had gotten on his boxing gloves, and from there it got into Clay's eyes.

Clay thought he was going blind. When he went back to his corner at the end of round four, he told Angelo that he couldn't see. Clay wanted to stop the fight. Angelo washed Clay's eyes with water and told him to calm down. When the bell rang to start round five, Angelo pushed Clay back into the fight.

"This is the big one!" Angelo told him. "Stay away from him! Run!"

Clay stayed away from Liston's fists. Then his eyes got clear and he could see again, so he began to fight back.

In round six, Clay took over the fight. He attacked all the time. Now Liston was too tired to do much. Clay just kept punching Liston. The bell rang and the round was over.

When the bell rang again for round seven to start, Sonny Liston didn't get up to fight. The fight was over. Clay had won. He was the world champ.

Clay ran around the ring with his arms up. "I am the greatest!" he yelled.

Chapter 5

Say My Name

Muhammad Ali told reporters that he had become a Muslim.

After the fight, Clay told the reporters that he had become a Muslim. He told them, "I believe in Allah and in peace. I'm not a Christian anymore. I don't have to be who you want me to be. I'm free to be who I want."

He also told them his new Muslim name. It was "Muhammad Ali."

Many whites were upset when Clay became Muhammad Ali. They didn't think that a Black Muslim should be allowed to be the champion of boxing.

Many black people didn't like Clay's new name either. They thought that the Nation of Islam caused trouble between the races. A lot of Black Muslims had been in prison. The Muslims trained themselves in fighting. Most blacks didn't think this was the best way to win respect.

Many people refused to call Ali by his new name. This was a way of insulting him. Later, those people changed their minds. They learned to love the name.

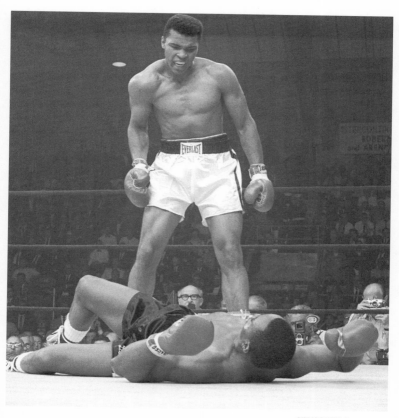

Cassius Clay stands over Sonny Liston after knocking him out in their fight.

But at that time, they couldn't get over their fear of the Nation of Islam.

Sonny Liston wanted a re-match with Ali. A lot of people still thought that Liston was a better boxer. They thought that Liston would win the next fight. The fight was held in May 1965. Ali came out swinging. He knocked Liston out in round one.

The next man who wanted to fight Ali was an old boxer named Floyd Patterson. Patterson had been a great boxer once.

He was too old to fight anymore, but he hated the Black Muslims. He didn't think that a Muslim should be the champ. Patterson still called Ali by his old name.

That made Ali angry. He called Patterson an "Uncle Tom." An Uncle Tom is a black man who does things just to please white people.

The fight was held in November 1965. Ali could have knocked Patterson out right away, but he didn't do it. He kept hitting Patterson without knocking him out.

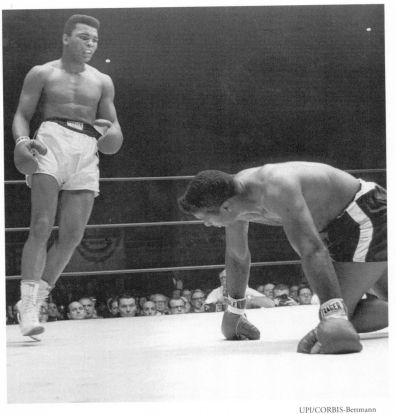

Muhammad Ali dances away from Floyd Patterson during their 12-round fight.

He tortured Patterson with punches. When the fight was over, the reporters were angry. They said that Ali had been cruel. They said that he was like a boy pulling the wings off a butterfly. But Ali thought the fight was about pride. People had to respect his religion. They had to call him by his name.

But something else was going on in the U.S. then. It was something more important than boxing. The U.S. was at war in Vietnam. Vietnam is a small country in Asia.

The country was divided into North Vietnam and South Vietnam. South Vietnam was at war with North Vietnam and the U.S. was on the side of South Vietnam. South Vietnam was also fighting against a group of South Vietnamese who were called the Viet Cong. Most Americans didn't know much about Vietnam but they did know that North Vietnam was a communist country. The U.S. said that all communist countries were bad, so at first most Americans thought that it was right to fight on the side of South Vietnam.

In 1966, the U.S. government was ordering young men in America to join the army. This was called the draft. In each state there was a draft board that chose the men who had to fight. If a man was chosen, he had to go. He didn't have any choice about it.

Ali's draft board decided to draft him, but the Nation of Islam was against joining the army. The Nation of Islam was against black people fighting wars that were run by white people.

In 1966, the U.S. government was ordering young men in America to join the army.

It was against the war in Vietnam because the Vietnamese were Asian. The Nation of Islam thought it was wrong for white men to send black men to kill Asians in Vietnam.

When Ali heard that he was going to be drafted, he told the reporters, "Man, I ain't got no quarrel with them Viet Cong."

Soon his words were in all the newspapers. Now even more people were angry at Ali.

They called him a traitor for speaking out against the war. Ali said he was not a traitor. He said that his religion told him not to kill people in a war.

Chapter 6

The King with No Crown

UPI/CORBIS-Bettmann

In 1967, Ali was put on trial because he wouldn't join the army.

In the United States, the law says that a man doesn't have to join the army if it's against his religion to kill people. The law also says that a minister of a church can't be drafted. Ali had become a minister of the Nation of Islam, so that was another reason that he shouldn't be drafted.

The draft board didn't agree with Ali. They wanted to send him to jail because he wouldn't join the army. Ali's lawyers went to court against the draft board to find out who was right.

But the courts can take a long time to decide things in the United States.

Meanwhile, lots of people were getting angry about Ali not joining the army. In fact, many states told him that he couldn't box in their state anymore. Soon Ali had to hold his boxing matches in other countries. That was a good thing for Ali in a way. In other countries, people were glad to see him. In fact, they were glad that he was against the war in Vietnam.

In April 1967, Ali was told that he had to go into the army. If he didn't, he would go to jail. But by this time, Ali was even more against the war.

He said, "Why should I go ten thousand miles from home and drop bombs on brown people when black people in Louisville are treated like dogs? If I thought that going to war would bring freedom to my people, I would join tomorrow. But I have to obey the laws of Islam. I have to follow my beliefs. I'll go to jail."

By this time, many Americans wanted Ali to go to jail. But many young people didn't want him to go. The war was getting bigger. Each month, more men were being drafted. Thousands of men were dying in Vietnam. Millions of Vietnamese people were getting killed, too. A lot of Americans thought that the war was wrong. They thought the army should come home.

In June 1967, Ali was put on trial. The court said that he would have to go to jail for five years.

Many college students were against the war in Vietnam.

Then the men who were in charge of pro boxing took away Ali's championship. They threw him out of boxing. Ali was only 25 years old. He had been champion of the world, but now he had lost his crown. Ali was not sent to jail right away. His lawyers appealed his case. In an appeal, a second court decides whether the first court was fair. It can take a long time to decide an appeal. Meanwhile, Ali was not in jail, but the government took away his passport so that he couldn't leave the U.S.

Muhammad Ali reads from the holy book called the Koran.

It took more than three years to decide the case. During that time, Ali was not allowed to box, but he still had to make a living. So he earned money by making speeches to college students. A lot of students wanted to hear him. He told them why he was against the war. He talked about freedom of religion. He talked about black pride. He spoke out against hate. He spoke out against drugs.

In those three years, the country changed its mind about the war. Now most people were against the war.

They thought that it was not helping anyone. They thought that the U.S. could never win the war. More than 35,000 U.S. soldiers had been killed. Some of the biggest leaders in the country were saying that we should stop the war. Ali had become a hero to millions of young people because he had stood up against the war.

Chapter 7

A Broken Jaw

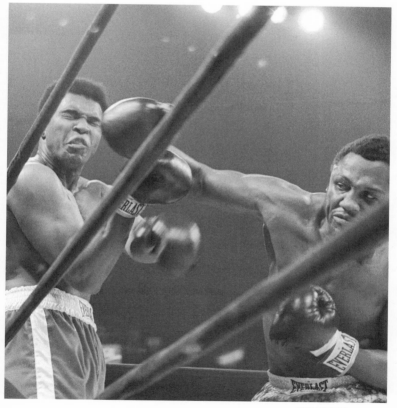

UPI/CORBIS-Bettmann

Joe Frazier punches Muhammad Ali during their
15-round fight.

In 1971, the U.S. court said that Ali had a right to work as a boxer so, in March, Ali fought to win back the heavyweight crown. The champion was a man named Joe Frazier.

There was lots of talk before the fight. Ali wanted everyone to be on his side. He talked about Joe Frazier like Joe Frazier was just another Uncle Tom. Ali said that Joe was a traitor to black people. Ali said that he was a better black man than Frazier. This made Frazier angry because he had worked hard all of his life.

He came from a very poor black family. But Joe Frazier wasn't a fast talker like Ali. Joe could fight with his fists, but he couldn't fight very well with words.

Ali had not been fighting for more than three years. He was older now. He was slower. Why did that matter so much? It mattered because he couldn't duck away from punches so fast anymore. He would probably get more beaten up in the boxing ring.

It was a hard fight. It lasted 15 rounds. Joe Frazier was tough. He pounded Ali's body.

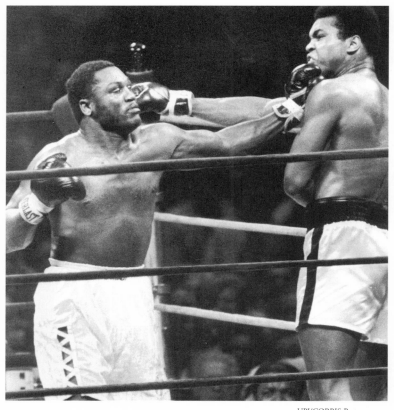

Muhammad Ali and Joe Frazier hit each other during their fight for the heavyweight title.

In round 15, Frazier hit Ali hard on the chin and Ali went down. He got up again right away, but he couldn't knock Joe Frazier down. In the end, the judges decided that Joe Frazier had won. Frazier was still the champ. He told reporters that he didn't think Ali wanted to fight him again.

Ali was quiet after the fight. He wasn't crowing like a rooster anymore.

The next day, a reporter came up to Ali and said, "Last night Joe Frazier told us that you wouldn't want to fight him again. Is that true?"

Ali smiled and said, "Oh, how wrong he is."

Three months later, the courts decided Ali's case against the draft board. The court said that Ali was right. He didn't have to go into the army and he didn't have to go to jail. He was free.

After losing to Joe Frazier, Ali fought a lot of other matches before he tried to be champ again. He won ten fights in a row. In round two of the next fight, his jaw was broken by a boxer named Ken Norton.

CORBIS/Bettmann-UPI

**Ken Norton punches Muhammad Ali in a fight in
March 1973.**

Ali lost the fight, but he showed how brave he was about pain. He had fought ten rounds with a broken jaw.

In six months, Ali's jaw healed. Then he went back and beat Ken Norton.

Chapter 8

The Comeback

UPI/CORBIS-Bettmann

Muhammad Ali trains for a fight.

In 1973, a man named George Foreman became the new champ. The next year, Ali got a chance to box against Foreman. Seven years had passed since Ali had lost the boxing crown. The fight was held in an African country called Zaire. Today that country is called Congo. All over the world, people watched the fight on TV. Before the fight, Ali made it sound like it was going to be fun. He made people laugh by saying, "George Foreman is nothing but a big mummy!"

But Foreman was not a big mummy. He was a bull. He was one of the strongest men that Ali ever fought. And Ali couldn't just dance away from punches anymore. Ali was going to get beaten up.

So in this fight, Ali tried a new plan. In the first rounds, he didn't even try to attack. He held up his arms to protect his head and let George Foreman beat on him. Ali leaned against the ropes while Foreman hit him. Ali tried to save his own strength. He wanted Foreman to get tired of punching.

UPI/CORBIS-Bettmann

George Foreman and Muhammad Ali fight for the world heavyweight title.

It hurt like heck, but Ali did that for six rounds. In round six, he could tell that Foreman's arms were getting tired. He started to talk to Foreman while they were fighting.

"Hit harder!" Ali told Foreman. "Show me something, George! You're not hurting me. What's wrong with you? I thought you said you were bad!"

Then Ali began to fight back. Each time that Foreman threw a punch, Ali threw a faster punch back at him.

In round eight, Foreman was chasing Ali around the ring. Suddenly, Ali hit him hard in the head. Foreman went down. He stayed down. He had worn himself out. He was just too tired to get up again. Ali had won by a knockout. After seven long years, Muhammad Ali was "the greatest" again.

Now Ali was treated differently. The Vietnam war was over. People didn't want to think about it anymore. They wanted to forget all the anger about the war.

UPI/CORBIS-Bettmann

George Foreman is too tired to get up after Muhammad Ali knocked him out.

More people began to love Ali again. Everyone could agree that he was a brave man. He had made a great comeback. He had lost his crown and then won it back. President Ford invited Ali to the White House. Now Ali was a national hero. He was also the most famous athlete in the world.

Chapter 9

Always Ali

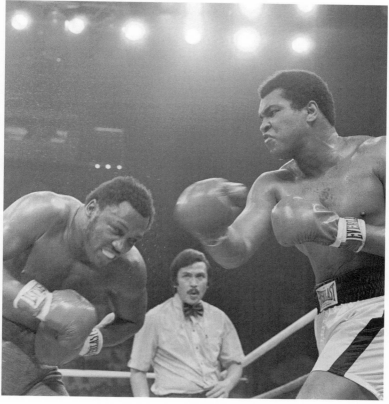

UPI/CORBIS-Bettmann

Muhammad Ali fights Joe Frazier in 1975.

No man can box forever. Ali kept boxing for seven more years, but that was too long. In 1975, he fought Joe Frazier again. They pounded each other for 14 rounds. They were both so tired that they could hardly move their arms. In round 15, Ali came out to fight, but Frazier just stayed in his corner. So Ali had won. Later he said, "Frazier quit just before I did. I didn't think I could fight anymore."

Boxing is a mean sport. When men get hit too much, it destroys their bodies and brains. Ali's doctor had told him that he should quit boxing.

Ali tried to quit boxing, but he couldn't do it. He loved being famous. In every fight, he made millions of dollars. He had already made a lot of money, but most of it was gone. He had bought a training camp in the country. He had to pay lawyers. He was giving money to a lot of people. He had given lots of money away to people who were in trouble.

He could never say no. Ali had also given money to people who said that they would invest it for him. These people promised to make his money grow, but they lost most of it. When people cheated Ali, he never stayed angry with them. At home, he was always a soft, big-hearted man. He always said, "I forgive you." His religion told him that people should forgive each other.

In 1975, the head of the Nation of Islam died. The new leader changed things.

Now the group didn't blame whites for all the problems of blacks. It didn't try to divide people by race so much.

Ali was glad about this change. He had never hated whites. Angelo Dundee was white. Ali and Angelo had always been friends. Ali said, "Hearts and souls have no color."

In 1978, Ali lost his crown to Leon Spinks. In 1980, he lost another fight. In 1981, he boxed one more time and lost again. He was 39 years old.

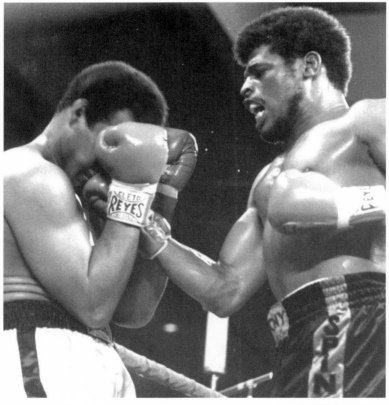

Muhammad Ali tries to protect his face as Leon Spinks punches him. Spinks won the fight in 15 rounds.

In a few years, Ali's body got worse. He could think, but he couldn't speak quickly. The doctors told him that he had been hit too many times. Nothing could make him better. Each year, he moved more slowly. He spoke more slowly. He couldn't even drive anymore. People had to do things for him that he had always done for himself.

Ali looked different now, also. His body was heavy and his face was like a mask that couldn't move. But on the inside, he was still Ali.

He didn't want pity. Each day, he went out with booklets about Islam and gave them to students. He still loved to meet and talk with people.

In 1996, the summer Olympic Games were held in Atlanta, Georgia. On the first night, a burning torch was carried onto the field. The torch was going to light the flame in the high Olympic tower. Thousands of people were there. Millions were watching on TV all over the world. Suddenly, they saw Muhammad Ali standing at the tower.

Muhammad Ali lights the flame at the 1996 Olympics in Atlanta, Georgia.

Someone handed him the torch and he lit the flame. In 1960, he had been just a young boxer who wanted to light up the sport of boxing. Now he was lighting a flame again for all the world to see.

After his boxing days were over, Ali said, "Maybe I was great in the ring. But outside of boxing, I'm just a brother like other people. I want to have a good life and serve God.

I want to help everybody I can. And one more thing. I'm still gonna find out who stole my bike. And I'm still gonna whup him. That was a good bike!"

The End

About the Start-to-Finish® Writer

Alan Venable was born in Pittsburgh, Pennsylvania, in 1944 and has lived and traveled in various parts of America, Africa, and Asia. In addition to his books in the Start-to-Finish series, he has written several books of fiction for children, school curricular texts, and plays and novels for adults. He lives in San Francisco where he enjoys walking the hills, exploring new music, and learning new languages.

About the Reader

Bernard Mixon is a professional actor who performs on the stage, in films, and in many television shows and commercials. On stage, Bernard has played the role of Julius Caesar at the Black Ensemble Theatre and the role of the lion in the popular play, *The Wiz.* You may have seen Bernard as Magic Sam in the 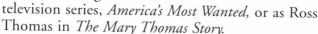 television series, *America's Most Wanted,* or as Ross Thomas in *The Mary Thomas Story.*

For the past ten years, Bernard has been singing jazz, pop, country and gospel music with a band called *The Moods.* When he performs with this group, he also plays the harmonica, drums and other kinds of percussion instruments.

A Note from the Start-to-Finish® Editors

This book has been divided into approximately equal short chapters so that the student can read a chapter and take the cloze test in one reading session. This length constraint has sometimes required the authors and editors to make transitions in mid-chapter or to break up chapters in unexpected places.

You will also notice that Start-to-Finish Books look different from other high-low readers and chapter books. The text layout of this book coordinates with the other media components (CD and audiocassette) of the Start-to-Finish series.

The text in the book matches, line for line and page for page, the text shown on the computer screen, enabling readers to follow along easily in the book. Each page ends in a complete sentence so that the student can either practice the page (repeat reading) or turn the page to continue with the story. If the next sentence cannot fit on the page in its entirety, it has been shifted to the next page. For this reason, the sentence at the top of a page may not be indented, signaling that it is part of the paragraph from the preceding page.

Words are not hyphenated at the ends of lines. This sometimes creates extra space at the end of a line, but eliminates confusion for the struggling reader.